The Trouble with Jack

SHIRLEY HUGHES

The Bodley Head

London

Once upon a time there was a little girl
called Nancy who lived in London

with her mother

and her father

and her little brother Jack.

3

Nancy was a tidy child who always knew where everything was kept. She often washed her dolls' clothes and liked brushing and combing their hair.

The trouble with Jack was that he was not a tidy person at all.

I am sorry to say that he was very messy and his table manners were awful. He threw his toys about all over the floor and walked on the furniture and stole treacle out of the tin. One day he found the big scissors and cut off the hair from Nancy's dolls. He thought it would grow again, but of course it wouldn't. They had to have new hair bought for them at a special shop.

When Nancy and her mother took
Jack for a walk in the park he would
seize the pushchair and run off in the
wrong direction pretending he was a
very fast express train. Once he gave
the pushchair a great shove downhill
so that it ran faster and faster and
splash! into a pond at the bottom.

Mother had to borrow a gentleman's walking stick to get it out.

9

Now the time was getting near to Nancy's birthday and she was very excited. Whenever they passed a toyshop she spent a long time pointing out all the things she hoped somebody would give her, until Jack got tired of this and tried to drag her on.

11

But even Jack was quite interested when the postman came to their house with some large parcels addressed to Nancy, with labels on them saying

NOT TO BE OPENED UNTIL NOVEMBER 27TH.

Mother put the parcels away
in a safe place where the children
could not find them,

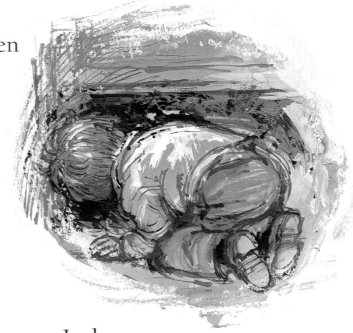

not even Jack,
who tried quite hard.

One morning very early, when Mother and Father were asleep, Nancy and Jack were playing on the sitting-room sofa. Nancy had piled up all the cushions to make a house but Jack kept bouncing and knocking them over.

"I'm a huge enormous man! Look, I'm a giant!" shouted Jack, balancing along the sofa back. From up there he could see on to the top of the cupboard and there, right at the back, were those interesting-looking brown paper parcels.

"There are your birthday presents! I can see the one
from Granny! Help me get it down, Nancy."

"Oh no, we mustn't," said Nancy, remembering the labels.
"It will spoil the surprise on my birthday."

But the parcels looked so exciting that she wanted very
much to know what was inside. She thought perhaps they
could just get off a corner of the paper and have a little peep.

16

Jack dragged up a chair to the cupboard and stood on it, but he could not reach the parcels. He fetched a stool and put it on the chair, but still he was not high enough. He fetched three cushions and piled them up on the stool.

Nancy helped him climb up.

When he was at the top, everything started to wobble and –

crash! down went Jack with a loud yell. He hurt his head badly enough to need a sticking plaster on it, and Nancy never saw inside the parcels. Mother put them away in an even safer place where nobody could find them.

Nancy and Jack soon forgot about looking for parcels because something very nice happened. Mother said that Nancy was to have a party on her birthday. Nancy helped write out some of the invitations to her friends and Jack posted them for her.

Then Mother was very busy indeed. She went shopping and bought some pretty material with roses all over it to make a party dress for Nancy. It had a frill round the collar and a red sash.

"What will Jack wear to be smart for the party?"
asked Nancy.

"He'll wear his best trousers."

Jack didn't seem to care much what he wore.
But he cared about the party tea.

Mother made a great many jellies and trifles and little iced cakes and a big birthday cake covered in white icing, with sugar violets and five pink candles. It had a lovely silver paper frill round it. There were to be potato crisps and chocolate finger biscuits and sausages on sticks too.

On Nancy's birthday morning her presents were piled up beside her plate. There was a glove puppet from Granny, a box of paints, a family of tiny teddies with a set of chairs just the right size for them to sit on, and a doll's saucepan from Jack.

Mother and Father gave her
a beautiful bride doll in a box.
She had golden hair and a
white satin dress. Also in the
box was a hat, another dress
for the doll to wear and a pair
of red boots.

All morning Nancy played with her presents, and Jack felt
in a not-liking-Nancy-very-much-mood until he found that
Granny had sent him a present of his own – a new car.

After lunch and rest were over Mother brought out a great many different coloured balloons and a box of crackers and some paper mugs and drinking straws. They blew up the balloons and hung up bunches of them in the sitting-room.

23

They set the table with a pretty cloth and put out all the delicious food, with a cracker beside each plate.

When all was ready Nancy thought she had never seen such a beautiful tea before, not even in picture books.

24

Mother said she would help Nancy to get ready for the party first and leave Jack until the last minute because he never stayed clean for very long.

"May I wear my sticking-out petticoat and my bracelet that Auntie Barbara gave me?" asked Nancy.

"Yes, if you like."

They left Jack playing on the stairs with his cars. But after a time he began to get bored with this. He saw that the sitting-room door was a little bit open, and he thought of all the lovely things that were inside. AND DO YOU KNOW WHAT HAPPENED NEXT?

Well, I am sure you can imagine.

27

When Nancy and her mother came downstairs and saw what Jack had done – the balloons pulled down, and the crackers opened with the surprises taken out and the silver frill pulled off the cake and all the pretty party table in a mess, Nancy burst into tears. Mother was *very* cross. Then Jack began to cry loudly too. How terrible it all was!

In the end Mother told them both to stop crying and wiped their noses.

"There's still a little time before the party children arrive. Perhaps if we all try hard we can make it all right again."

Jack was now very sorry about what he had done. He ran to help Nancy fetch the broom and dustpan, and helped to pick up all the things off the floor. Some of the little cakes were squashed and had to be thrown away, but there were still plenty left and the big cake looked all right when they put back its silver paper frill. They hung up the bunches of balloons just as before, and luckily Mother found some spare crackers in the box.

So Nancy had her birthday party after all. There was the lovely tea and afterwards they played "Oranges and Lemons" and "Nuts in May" and musical bumps and there was a balloon and a present for each child to take home.

Jack enjoyed the party as much as anyone, and was so good and happy that they had to forgive him.

"The trouble with Jack," said Nancy at bedtime, "is that as he's my brother I've got to put up with him whatever he's like."

Published by Random House Children's Books
20 Vauxhall Bridge Road, London SWIV 2SA
A division of Random House UK Ltd
London Melbourne Sydney Auckland
Johannesburg and agencies throughout the world
Copyright © Shirley Hughes 1970
1 3 5 7 9 10 8 6 4 2
First published by The Bodley Head Children's Books 1970
Set in Berkeley
Printed and bound in Singapore
RANDOM HOUSE UK Limited Reg. No. 954009